The ADVENTURES of

Kirra & Rincon

Where's the Beach?

Li'l Kids, Big Waves

by **Shelley & Justin Kerr**

illustrated by **Rick Hemphill**

Published by Kirra & Rincon Enterprises

Kirra awoke, grabbed her bags,
And headed for the door.
She was excited to leave Australia,
For the California shore.

Her cousin Rincon lived there,
They planned to surf and swim;
She knew that once she boarded the plane,
Her adventure would begin.

Flying above the ocean blue,
The land below looked small.
There were so many islands,
Kirra couldn't count them all.

She gazed at the Pacific,
Amazed by what she'd seen,
The thousands of little islands
Looked so beautiful, lush, and green.

At the airport Rincon waited,
  With sunscreen, surfboards, and wax.
Before they headed for the coast,
  They bought some healthy snacks.

Rincon wanted some crackers and cheese,
  Kirra just wanted a peach;
They ate their snacks in front of the store,
  Then headed for the beach.

Cruising up the highway,
 The ocean sparkling in the sun;
Every surf spot they passed,
 Looked exciting, inviting, and fun.

They drove a little further,
    Grabbed their boards, and jumped right in.
While floating through the waves,
    They couldn't help but grin.

As they waited patiently
    For the perfect wave to ride,
Mother nature sent a gift—
    Some dolphins by their side.

The ocean was their playground,
There were no slides or swings.
Just some dolphins having fun,
Flying through the waves without wings.

Inspired by their style,
  Kirra paddled for the swell.
She stood to her feet,
  And then she nearly fell.

Rincon hurried towards her,
  Then he saw that she was fine.
So he turned to the wave,
  And rode it down the line.

The waves were getting bigger;
  They were pounding on the shore.
Kirra was so afraid;
  She couldn't see Rincon anymore.

She turned to face the ocean;
A wall of water was all she could see.
Holding tightly to her surfboard,
She was as scared as she could be.

Although she saw a huge wave
  That was nearly twice her size,
She spun around and paddled hard,
  Then finally closed her eyes.

She felt the board begin to glide;
  Her heart just skipped a beat.
She said, "It's either now or never,"
  Then jumped up to her feet.

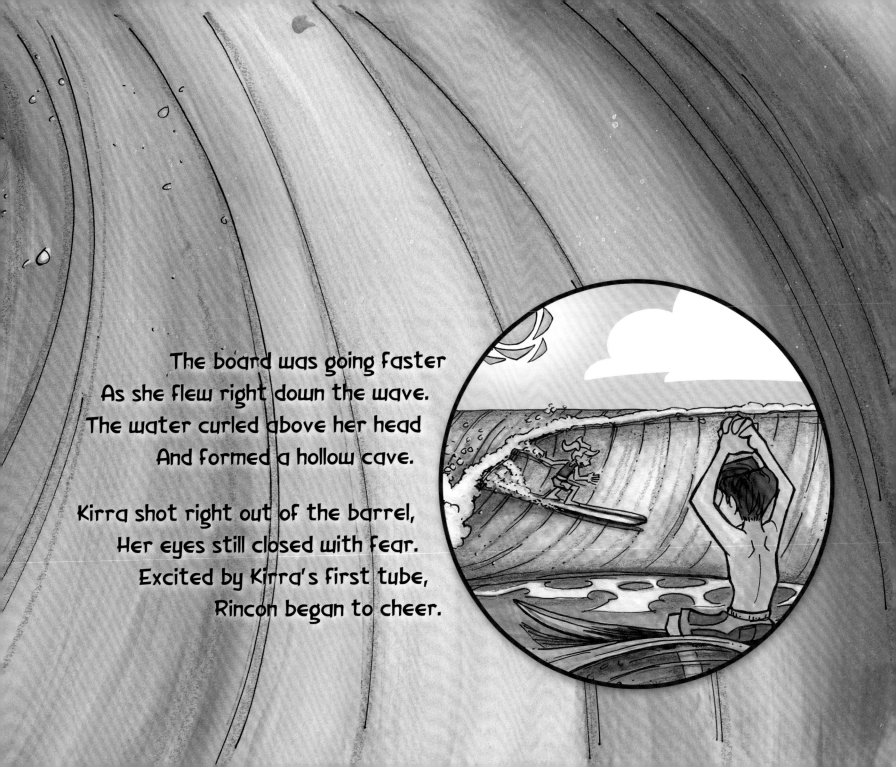

The board was going faster
As she flew right down the wave.
The water curled above her head
And formed a hollow cave.

Kirra shot right out of the barrel,
Her eyes still closed with fear.
Excited by Kirra's first tube,
Rincon began to cheer.

Rincon said, "How could this happen?
    I've waited through the years,
For the perfect wave that you just caught,
    After facing all your fears."

Kirra smiled from ear to ear,
She felt so proud and brave.
She never thought in a million years,
That SHE'd catch the perfect wave.

Kirra and Rincon continued to surf
Throughout that summer day.
They surfed until the sun went down,
Then they were on their way.

Before they left the beach,
  They lent a helping hand
By picking up their trash,
  Leaving only footprints in the sand.

Surfing was their hobby,
   But they learned much more that season.
Whether the waves were big or small,
   They were happy for many reasons.

Happiness was the ocean breeze,
The warm sand under their feet;
The special times they spent with friends,
And others that they meet.

Place
Your
Photo
Here

This Book Belongs To:

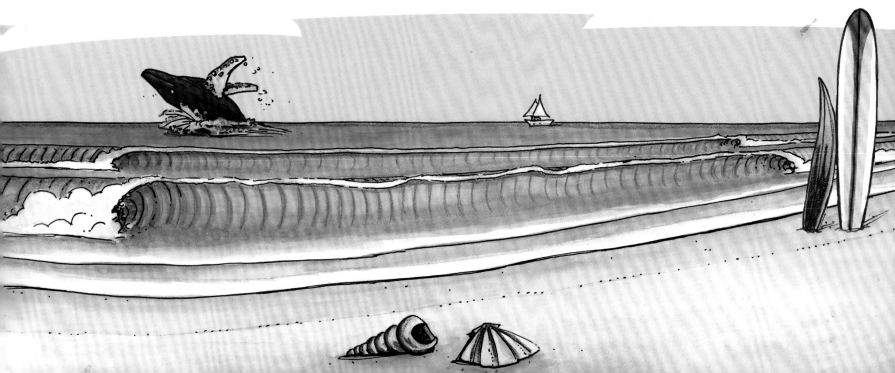

Where in the World Are Kirra & Rincon?

UNITED STATES of AMERICA

CHINA

PHILIPPINES

INDONESIA   NEW GUINEA

SOLOMON IS.

AUSTRALIA

PACIFIC OCEAN
[World's Largest Ocean!]

HAWAII, U.S.A.

Kirra flew over 7,450 miles (12,066 km) to California!

VANUATU

SAMOA

FIJI

NEW CALEDONIA

TAHITI

MARQUESAS

RINCON POINT
California, U.S.A.

Rincon is named after one of California's finest point breaks. Rincon Point is located near Santa Barbara, California. The waves at Rincon allow very long rides with surfers performing many turns, moves and sometimes riding in the tube.

? Rincon has a pet iguana named Cojo (CO-HO). What are the some silly things that Cojo does in the story?

? Do you like to travel? Did you know most surfers like to travel to surf on different waves?

KIRRA POINT
Queensland, Australia

Kirra is named after a world famous sandy bottom point break wave located on the Gold Coast of Queensland, Australia. Kirra Point has very fast-riding waves, many allowing the surfers to ride in the tube.

? Koala bears are from Australia. How many times do you see Kirra's stuffed koala bear in the story? Have you ever seen a real koala bear?

NEW ZEALAND

? Kirra flew over thousands of islands on her way to California. Can you find New Zealand, Australia, Tahiti, Fiji, and Hawaii on the map? All of these islands have great places to surf.

TASMANIA

Types of Surfboards:

This is a LONGboard!
[Kirra rides a longboard]

A surfboard that has a round nose at the front and can be over 9 feet long. The first modern surfers rode long boards made of wood in the early 1900s. Today longboards are made of foam and fiberglass.

Longboards are fun in smaller surf (2-6 feet) and are great for learning how to surf.

This is a SHORTboard!
[Rincon rides a shortboard]

A surfboard that has a pointed shaped nose and is normally closer to the height of the surfer (5 ft to 7ft). Shortboards were developed and first ridden in the late 1960s and early 1970s. Shortboards are also made of foam and fiberglass and lighter than longboards.

Shortboards allow quick turns and fast moves and are fun to ride in medium to large waves (4-10feet).

The RAIL:
The outside edge of the surfboard.

Tail FINS:
Help the board glide through the water!

Did You Know?

? DOLPHINS like to play in the waves. Dolphins are very smart and friendly animals. How many dolphins can you find in the story? Can you name the other animals that you see?

? "WOODY" is the nickname for a car made out of wood. Surfers liked to drive these cars because all their friends and surfboards could fit inside. It is the type of car that Kirra and Rincon ride in. Have you ever seen a car made out of wood? How many friends can you fit in your car?

? HEALTHY FOODS give you energy to surf and play. Kirra and Rincon like to eat healthy snacks. What is your favorite healthy snack?

? POINT BREAK is a shoreline that sticks out from the surrounding coastline forming a point. Waves break in the same shape from the tip all the way to the bottom of the point. The consistent shape of the waves allows the surfers to perform many moves with grace and style.

? TUBE or BARREL is the section of a wave that forms an area where the surfer can ride inside. Most tube rides last for just a few exciting seconds.

Surf to our website at
KirraandRincon.com

The ADVENTURES of

Li'l Kids, Big Waves

Kirra & Rincon

by **Shelley & Justin Kerr**

illustrated by **Rick Hemphill**

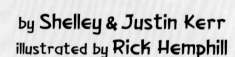

Kirra & Rincon Enterprises.
Atascadero, California
www.KirraandRincon.com

First Published by Kirra & Rincon Enterprises
The Adventures of Kirra & Rincon, Li'l Kids, Big Waves
Text copyright © 2005, by Shelley & Justin Kerr
Illustration copyright © 2005, by Rick Hemphill
All Rights Reserved.

ISBN 0-9766408-0-5
First Edition Printed in Hong Kong

This book is a collaboration between Kirra & Rincon Enterprises and Laughing Pencil Studio.
Book design by Rick Hemphill—www.laughingpencil.com.

The text of this book is set in **Gorilla Milkshake**, created by Nate Piekos—www.blambot.com
The illustrations are rendered in gouache, colored pencil, and ink on Strathmore 400lb. Vellum Bristol.

Shelley and Justin
Surfing in Southern California

About the Authors:

Shelley and Justin Kerr are married and live on the Central Coast of California. Shelley is an elementary school teacher and enjoys every opportunity to inspire children. Justin works in the food processing industry and spends his free time surfing and shaping longboards for close friends and family. The Tale of Kirra and Rincon was inspired by Justin and Shelley's love of the ocean, surfing and the peace of mind found while enjoying the beach.

Dedicated with all our love to our son Donovan. Thanks to our family for their love and support as we follow our dreams. Thanks cousin Rick for the wonderful illustrations. For all our new friends, we hope you'll find the beaches clean and peaceful wherever you may travel. —Shelley & Justin

Rick Hiking Buffalo Peaks
in the Colorado Rockies

About the Illustrator:

Rick Hemphill spent much of his boyhood in front of a sketchbook with pencil in hand. He now makes his living as one of those "starving artists" you were warned about in school—designing and illustrating all manner of stuff—and lovin' it! A native of Southern California, Rick has left the surf and sand for the Rocky Mountains of Colorado, where he lives with wife, Becky, their three girls (who have been known to run off with his erasers), Rusty the dog, Edgar the cat, and his Mac.

For Kiera, Brynnae, and Shaelyn, luv ya! Welcome to the world Donovan! Thanks Mom & Dad for your years of support. To Becky for your love, support, and our life together. Ultimate thanks to God for the gift. —Rick

the End.